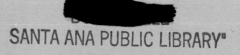
The Rabbit,
the Fox,
and
the Wolf

The Rabbit, the Fox, and the Wolf

by SARA

ORCHARD BOOKS ▪ New York

Copyright © 1990 by Sara
First American Edition 1991 published by Orchard Books
First published in France by Éditions Épigones

Orchard Books
A division of Franklin Watts, Inc.
387 Park Avenue South
New York, NY 10016

Manufactured in the United States of America
Printed by General Offset Company, Inc.
Bound by Horowitz/Rae
Book design by Susan Phillips

The illustrations are cut paper printed in full color.
10 9 8 7 6 5 4 3 2 1

Library of Congress Cataloging-in-Publication Data
Sara.
[Dans la gueule du loup. English]
The rabbit, the fox, and the wolf / by Sara. — 1st American ed.
p.   cm.
Translation of: Dans la gueule du loup.
Summary: After a rabbit, chased by a fox, is saved by a wolf,
the rabbit and the wolf become friends.
ISBN 0-531-05953-7. — ISBN 0-531-08553-8 (lib. bdg.)
[1. Rabbits—Fiction.   2. Wolves—Fiction.
3. Friendship—Fiction.   4. Stories without words.]
I. Title.
PZ7.S239Rab   1991
[E]—dc20   90-32443

The Rabbit,
the Fox,
and
the Wolf

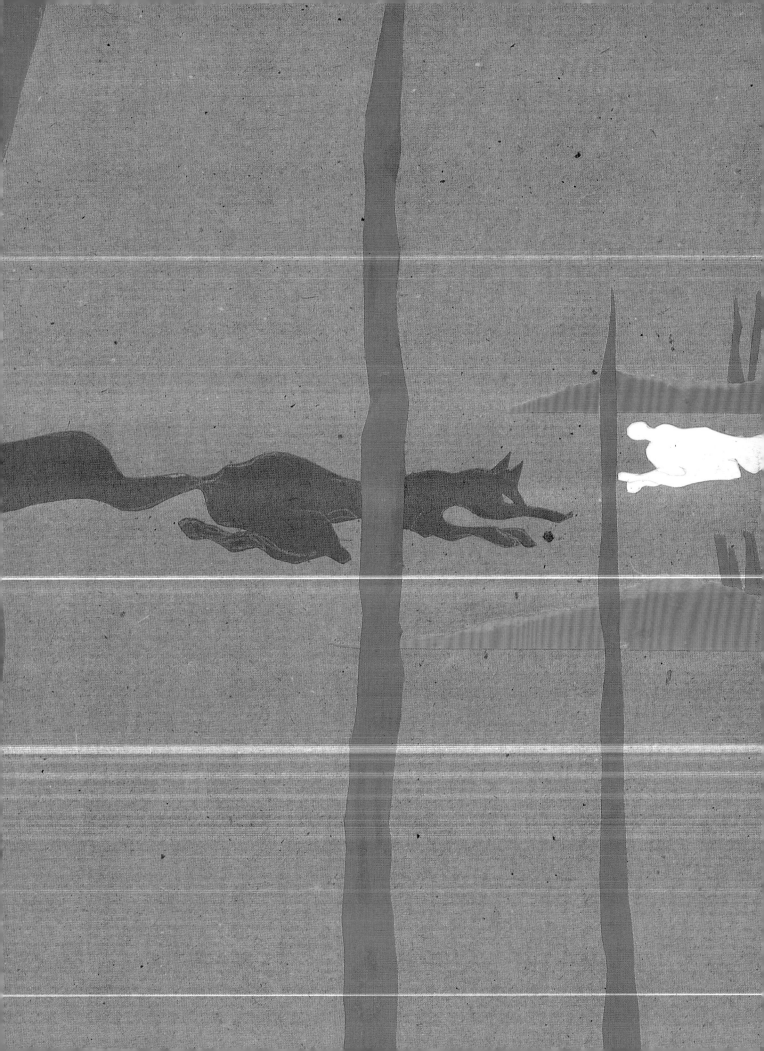